P9-DDE-809

First published in Japan in 1982 by Shiko-Sha Co., Ltd., Tokyo, under the title *Yoruno Tomodachi*.
Published in the United States, Great Britain, Canada, Australia, and New Zealand in 2010 by North-South Books Inc.,
an imprint of NordSüd Verlag AG, CH-8005 Zürich, Switzerland.
Distributed in the United States by North-South Books Inc., New York 10001.
Library of Congress Cataloging-in-Publication Data is available.
ISBN: 978-0-7358-2310-5 (trade edition).
Printed in China by Toppan Leefung Packaging & Printing Co., Ltd., Dongguan, P.R.C., March 2010
1   3   5   7   9 • 10   8   6   4   2

www.northsouth.com

Kazuo Iwamura

BEDTIME in the FOREST

NorthSouth
New York / London

"Time to get up!" Mama Squirrel called to her children, just like she did every morning.

Mick sat up in his bed and rubbed his eyes.

"I'm still sleepy," said Mack, and he rolled over and curled back up.

"Why do we always have to get up in the morning?" said Molly, yawning.

"Because I said so," said Mama. "Good squirrel children sleep at night and get up in the morning."

The sun was already high in the sky.
"What a beautiful day to play in the
treetops," said Mama.
"Yes!" the children agreed.

The children were hopping
through the trees when they happened
on an owl family.

"Look!" cried Mick. "The owls are still sleeping!"

"They must not be very good children," said Molly.

"Get up!" called Mack. "Come out and play with us!"

"Shhhh," said Mother Owl. "Owls sleep during the day.
Come back at night if you want to play."

"We saw owls sleeping in the daytime,"
Mick told Mama and Papa that night.
"They don't get up till nighttime,"
said Molly.

"Can we go play with them after supper?" asked Mack.

"No, no," said Mama. "After supper, it's your bedtime."

"You can play again tomorrow," said Papa.

"Good night," said Mama. "Sleep tight."
And she went back downstairs.

"Are you sleepy?" Mick whispered.

"Not a bit," whispered Mack.

"Let's go see the owls!" whispered Molly.

"Yes! Let's go!"

Quietly, the children hopped out their bedroom window and headed for the owl hole. The bright moon lit their way.

"It's almost as light as day," said Molly.

"It's nice being out at night," said Mack.

"Hi!" said Molly. "We've come to play with you!"
Soon the owl and squirrel children were good friends.
"Wow!" said Mick. "This is fun!"
"I want to try the rope swing too!" said Molly.
"Me too!" said Mack.

But before long, the squirrel
children got very tired and they fell asleep.
"What's wrong?" the owls wondered.
"Why are you sleeping? It's night—time to
play!" The owls were disappointed.

Luckily, Father Squirrel was out looking for his children.

"Oh, there you are!" he said. "Wake up, you naughty little squirrels. It's time to go home to bed."

"Oh my," said Mama. "Where have you been all this time?"

"They were playing with the owls,"
said Papa, "just as we thought."

The next morning, the children were late for breakfast.
"You must not go out to play at night again," said Mama.
"No," said Mick. "We won't do that again."
"The owls are wide-awake at night," said Mack. "But we got so sleepy."
"Good squirrel children sleep at night," said Molly.

"What are you making?" asked Mama.

"A mailbox for our friends the owls," said Mick.

"We miss them," said Mack.

"We can't play with them at night, so we'll
write letters to them in the daytime," said Molly.
"What a good idea!" said Mama.

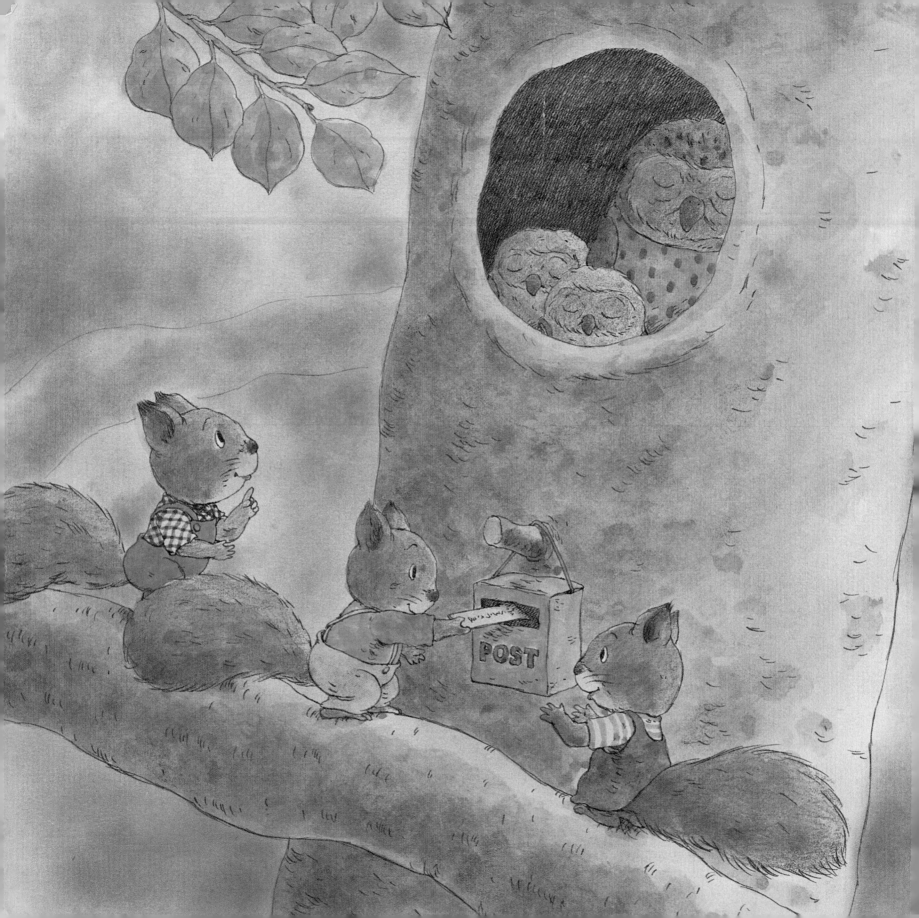

"Shhhh," said Mack. "The owls are sleeping."

"They'll find our letter tonight," Mick whispered.

"And tomorrow we'll get a letter back from them," whispered Molly.